THE TWENTY-FIVE MIXTEC CATS

MATTHEW GOLLUB

ART BY LEOVIGILDO MARTÍNEZ

TORTUGA PRESS
SANTA ROSA, CALIFORNIA

Tortuga Press
PMB: 181 2777 Yulupa Avenue
Santa Rosa, California 95405 U.S.A. Tel. 707-544-4720
The full-color illustrations were painted in watercolor on textured paper.
Printed in China

Produced by Matthew Gollub
Cover design by Karen Hanke

Library of Congress Cataloging-in-Publication Data

Gollub, Matthew. The twenty-five Mixtec cats/by Matthew Gollub;
illustrated by Leovigildo Martinez —Rev. ed. p. cm.
Summary: The inhabitants of a mountain village are suspicious of
the twenty-five cats who come to live with their healer, until the
cats are able to help lift a curse placed on the butcher.
[1. Cats—Fiction.   2. Mexico—Fiction.   3. Magic—Fiction.]
I. Martinez, Leovigildo, ill. II. Title.
PZ7.G583Tw 2004 [E] — dc22
Hardcover ISBN 10: 1-889910-28-7 ISBN 13: 978-1-889910-28-4
Paperback ISBN 10: 1-889910-29-5 ISBN 13: 978-1-889910-29-1
2   3   4   5   6   7   8   9   10

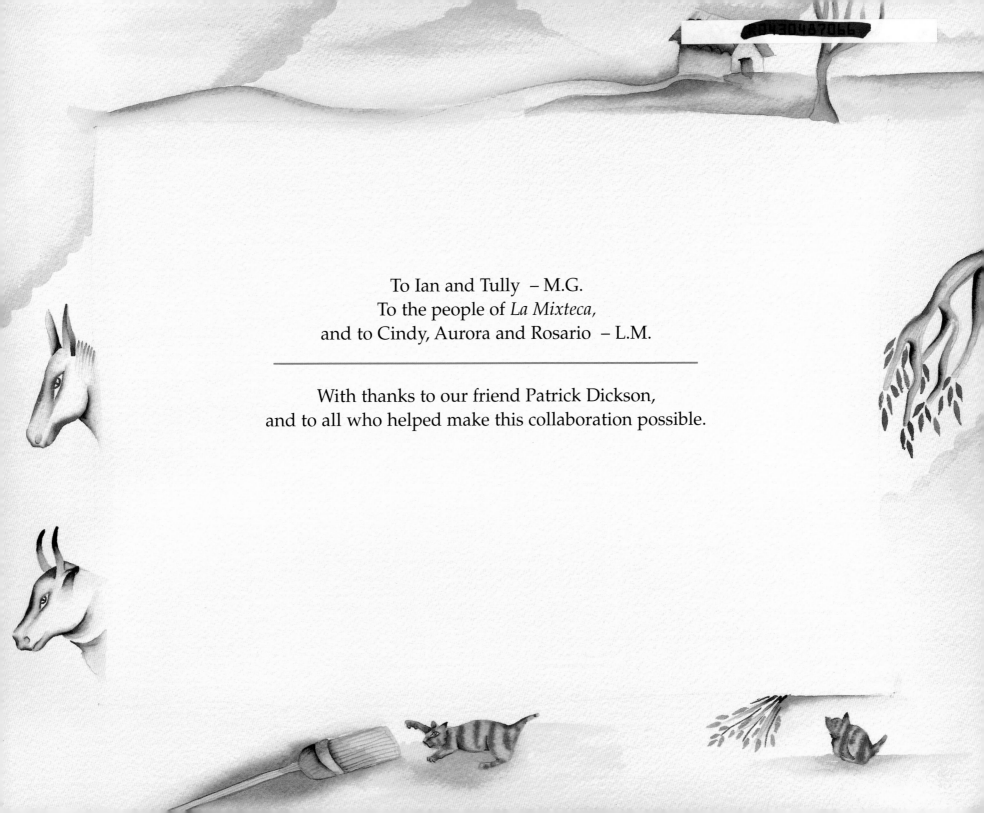

To Ian and Tully – M.G.
To the people of *La Mixteca*,
and to Cindy, Aurora and Rosario – L.M.

With thanks to our friend Patrick Dickson,
and to all who helped make this collaboration possible.

There once was a healer who lived alone in a village high in the mountains. You would never see any cats in his village. Not a single one lived there, for it was hot during the day, cold at night, and dusty all the time. It was not a comfortable place for cats—or for anyone else.

It was the healer's job to care for the sick. He would swish and swoosh fragrant herbs over their heads and sweep their illnesses away.

The people of the village depended on the healer and called for him quite often. But since the healer considered it his duty to help, he never asked for money. His patients would pay him with beans or corn, or with a little bit of change that was never enough.

One day, the healer went to a Mixtec market where a woman offered to give him twenty-five kittens. Since the healer was always short of money, and since no one in his village had ever had a cat, he carried the kittens home in a pillowcase to sell them door to door.

"How could we raise a cat?" scoffed his neighbors. "It's so hot and cold and dusty here. Besides, we don't have food for cats. It's hard enough just to feed our children."

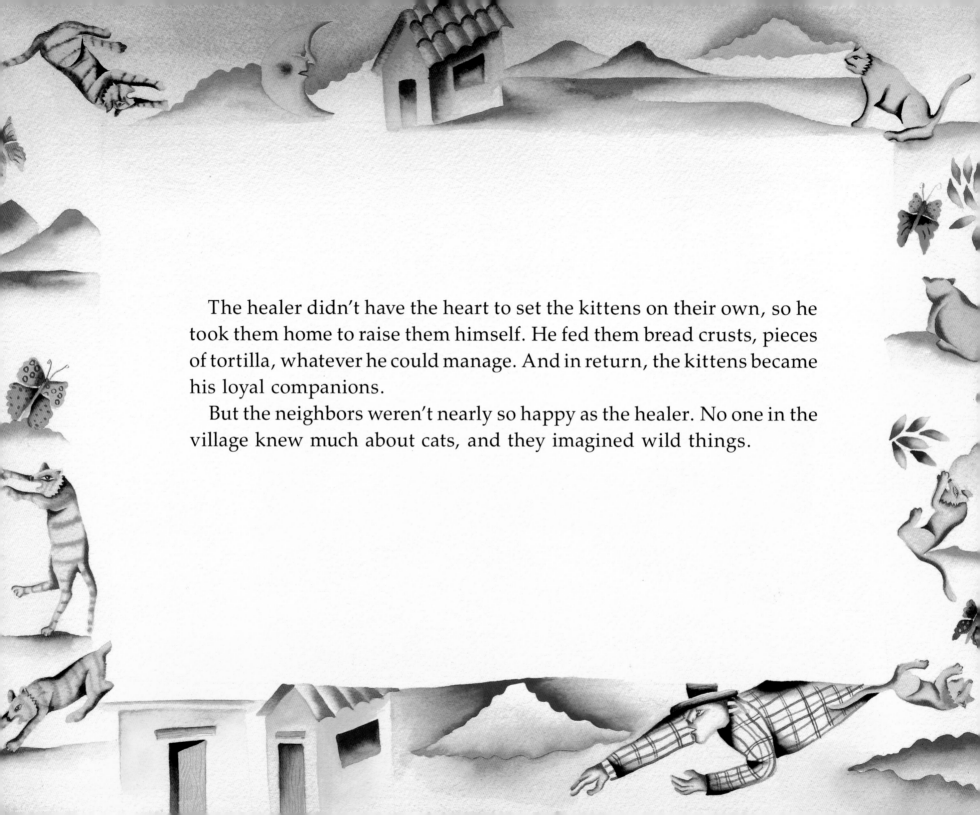

The healer didn't have the heart to set the kittens on their own, so he took them home to raise them himself. He fed them bread crusts, pieces of tortilla, whatever he could manage. And in return, the kittens became his loyal companions.

But the neighbors weren't nearly so happy as the healer. No one in the village knew much about cats, and they imagined wild things.

"They'll eat all my flour," bemoaned the baker, "then how will I go about baking bread?"

"Cats don't eat flour," said the butcher woman. "They eat mice, but also cows!"

"And to keep warm at night," cried the hatmaker and the florist, "they'll set fire to our fields!"

The neighbors marched to the healer's home and pounded on the door. "You must get rid of those filthy rodents," pronounced the butcher. "They make too much noise. We've heard the way they meow. And it's only a matter of time before they eat up all our food."

The healer felt it was important to get along with his neighbors. "The kittens will stay by my side," he promised. "They won't cause any trouble."

Soon the healer was known for his helpers, the twenty-five Mixtec cats. The kittens, which were growing up, learned to help him swish and swoosh. But still the neighbors gossiped by the well.

"Have you seen how big the cats have grown?"

"At this rate, they'll soon be the size of *burros*!"

"The cats are evil!" wailed the butcher. "So we must go to the evil healer!"

The evil healer lived outside the village. She lived all alone, the way the good healer used to, but devoted herself to very different work. It was this healer's business to cast evil spells.

When the neighbors paid her to get rid of the cats, she looked over her collection of magic things: poisonous herbs, a toucan's beak, even the skeleton of a rattlesnake. "No," she reconsidered. "I'll send messengers. That way no one will know I was responsible."

That night she flew through a haunted wood in search of her coyotes. She pointed toward where the healer lived, and the pack trotted off as if in a trance.

The good healer didn't wake up when the coyotes crept close. The coyotes stopped in front of his door and pointed their noses up in the air. They heard a meow from the north side of the house and loped through the dark. When they heard a meow from the south they rushed toward that sound, their jaws eager to snap. Next they heard the cries from the east and west, then from the north and south again! Soon the baffled coyotes were charging round and round the house until they grew so exhausted they dragged themselves back to the woods. The cats had taken turns meowing—while huddled safely on top of the roof.

The next morning when the cats followed the healer out to his field, the neighbors could not believe their eyes.

The butcher led the neighbors back to the evil healer. "We demand our money," she announced.

The evil healer tilted her head. "What nonsense is this?"

"You're nothing but a fake," said the butcher. "You can't even do away with twenty-five cats! You have no special powers."

The evil healer thrust her twisted fingers forward and glared into the butcher's eyes.

"We'll see who has no special powers," she menaced.

The following day, the butcher fell ill. The pain began with an ache in her gut. Then she felt flashes of hot and cold. She felt so dizzy that the meats in her stall began spinning before her eyes. She closed the stall and went home to lie down and couldn't get up for a day.

Two days passed and she didn't feel better. Her fever would not break, and she started to grow gaunt. The neighbors knew that unless they got help the butcher would not recover. They went to the good healer's home and described the sickness.

"It is hard," he said, "to cure a person of a curse. But, it is my duty to try."

The healer arrived at the butcher's home with his twenty-five cats. He arranged his sacred water, rosemary, and rue, while the cats swept out the house. He sprinkled the herbs with drops of the water and began to swish and swoosh. He and the cats repeated the process, but the butcher only moaned.

"Cats," the healer told them, "my powers alone are not enough. All of you must do as I do if we are to rid the butcher of evil."

The healer got the cats in position. Then, at his signal, he and the cats inhaled. They drew in a breath of air so hard it rustled the butcher's hair. As they held the breath of air in their mouths, the butcher began to recover! Color returned to her pallid face, and the pain in her gut was lifted!

"Bravo!" shouted the neighbors.

But then they noticed the healer's face. He could not exhale. The evil had left the butcher but now was stuck inside *him*! The cats, who were much smaller, could spit out the evil and continue to breathe. But the healer's cheeks were fast turning blue. Who would heal the healer?

The butcher got up to let the healer lie down. The neighbors looked on helplessly as the healer's hair turned gray and limp.

Suddenly, one cat leapt out the window and, in an eye's wink, ran to the evil healer's house. He snatched the evil healer's mask off her table and slipped out the door before she could shout.

He dragged it back to the home of the butcher. The other cats helped
him pull it onto the roof. They dropped the clay mask over the ledge and
watched it shatter on the ground.

At that instant the healer, sprawled on the mat, let out a tremendous
gasp of air. His breath created a gust of wind that whipped around the
room and wafted out the window.

The neighbors cheered with great relief. The cats had not only helped the butcher but saved the healer as well.

The butcher, florist, hatmaker, and baker now accepted them once and for all.

The Mixtec cats became heroes in the village as word of their brave deeds spread. To this day, the butcher gives them scraps of meat, and the baker feeds them bread. And the Mixtec cats play by the healer's side and make sure his house is clean.

LEOVIGILDO MARTÍNEZ lives in his native Oaxaca (wa-HAH-ka), a state in southern Mexico known for its artistic traditions. Oaxaca has seventeen ethnic minorities. Many, such as the Mixtecs, speak different languages to this day. This unusual mix of so many indigenous cultures has created a remarkable array of art, folklore and crafts. Fiestas, folk customs and even the textiles of the region find their way into Mr. Martínez's paintings, contributing to a genre that he describes as "figurative magic."

As a fine artist, Mr. Martínez has gained a worldwide following. His paintings from this book have been exhibited at over twenty-five museums around the United States. He now displays paintings in his own new gallery, *Púrpura Arte Actual*, located in the city of Oaxaca. Samples of his fine art may be viewed in the United States at Café Pasqual's Gallery in Santa Fe, New Mexico, and online at www.folkart.com/leo.

MATTHEW GOLLUB lives in Santa Rosa, California. He met Mr. Martínez while traveling in Oaxaca and, inspired by their friendship, began writing for young people. While researching this story, he visited healers and hiked through remote mountain villages. His subsequent collaborations with Mr. Martínez include *The Moon Was at a Fiesta* and *Uncle Snake* which, like this book, are available in Spanish.

Mr. Gollub's fluency in Spanish and Japanese has infused his picture books with unique perspectives. Two of his award-winning books—*The Jazz Fly* and *Gobble, Quack, Moon*—contain his musical narrations on audio CD. A dynamic speaker and advocate for family literacy, he speaks each year at over fifty schools and conferences nationwide and abroad. To learn more about Mr. Gollub and his acclaimed books, please visit www.matthewgollub.com.